KU-295-266

RUFUS
and the
BLACKBERRY MONSTER

To my dad

First published in the UK in 1999 by Piccadilly Press Ltd,
part of the Bonnier Publishing Group,
The Plaza, 535 King's Road, London, SW10 0SZ

www.bonnierpublishing.com

Text and illustration copyright © 1999 by Lisa Stubbs

1 3 5 7 9 10 8 6 4 2

All rights reserved. No part of this publication may be reproduced, stored in a retrieval system,
or transmitted, in any form or by any means electronic, mechanical, photocopying or
otherwise, without prior permission of the copyright owner.

The right of Lisa Stubbs to be recognised as Author of this work has been
asserted by her in accordance with the Copyright, Designs and Patents Act 1988.

ISBN 978-1-78370-566-5

Designed by Judith Robertson

Printed in Malaysia

RUFUS
and the
BLACKBERRY MONSTER

Lisa Stubbs

Piccadilly Press • London

"Rufus and Archie," said Mrs Fox,
"I'm going to bake a pie for Amber's birthday tea.
I need you to pick some blackberries.
Off you go!"

Rufus loved blackberry pie, but he didn't like
the blackberry bush at the bottom of the garden.
It was BIG and DARK and SCARY!
"Be brave, Rufus," said Mrs Fox.
"Fill your bucket right up to the brim!"

As they walked down the garden path,
Archie teased Rufus.

"The Blackberry Monster is hiding in the bush!"

"The Blackberry Monster!" said Rufus. His teeth
began to chatter. "Who's the Blackberry Monster?
He sounds very s-s-scary."

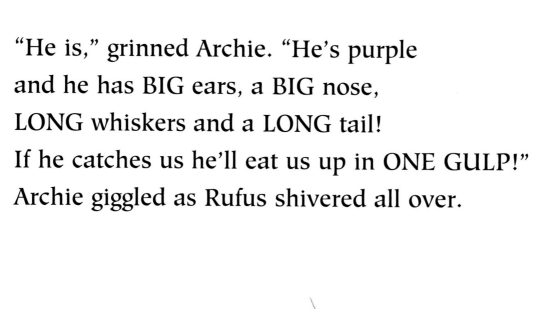

"He is," grinned Archie. "He's purple
and he has BIG ears, a BIG nose,
LONG whiskers and a LONG tail!
If he catches us he'll eat us up in ONE GULP!"
Archie giggled as Rufus shivered all over.

The blackberry bush loomed up ahead of them.

"You start here," said Archie in a bossy voice.

"I'll pick on the other side."

He sniggered as he disappeared.

He had taken the sunny side for himself.

Rufus was left alone in the darkest part
of the bush.

"I MUST be brave,"
thought Rufus.

He picked the blackberries
faster and faster.

Ping! Ping! Ping!
They flew into his bucket.

Rustle, crackle, rustle, snap! went a noise.
Rufus turned around. There was nothing there.

Rustle, rustle, crackle, snap!
Rufus's ears pricked up with fright.
"Archie, is that you?" he called. There was no
answer. Rufus *knew* it was the Blackberry Monster.
Maybe he should just run back home,
and forget about being brave!

Rustle, crackle, rustle, snap!
The monster was getting closer.
Rufus saw a dark shadow with BIG ears, a BIG nose,
LONG whiskers and a LONG tail . . .

Suddenly Archie rushed out from behind the bush.

He wasn't laughing any more.

"It's the Blackberry Monster!" he yelled.

"It's coming to eat us up!"

Archie was so scared he tried to hide behind Rufus.
But Rufus remembered to be brave –
brave enough for both of them!
The shadow was getting BIGGER and BIGGER
and CLOSER and CLOSER . . .

Rufus took a deep breath and shouted,
"I'm not scared of you!"
"Eeeeek!" cried the Blackberry Monster.
There in front of Rufus was a little, tiny, squeaky . . .

. . . mouse!

Rufus started to giggle. "It's all right, Archie, you can
look now. I've caught the Blackberry Monster!"
"Monster?" squeaked the mouse. "I'm not a monster.
I thought YOU were monsters!
I was so scared I dropped all my blackberries.
I haven't anything for my supper now."

"Then you'd better come home with us to
Amber's birthday tea. There'll be plenty to eat,"
said Rufus. He smiled at Archie.
Archie did his best to smile back.

Mrs Fox made the most extra delicious blackberry pie
for Amber's birthday tea. Rufus, Archie, Amber
and the tiny mouse ate it up in seconds.
Then Rufus told everyone about the Blackberry
Monster, and how brave he had been.
"I know who the Blackberry Monster is,"
said Mrs Fox, as she looked at their faces . . .

"You're ALL Blackberry Monsters!"